Dear Parents:

Congratulations! Your child is taking the first steps on an exciting journey. The destination? Independent reading!

STEP INTO READING® will help your child get there. The program offers five steps to reading success. Each step includes fun stories and colorful art or photographs. In addition to original fiction and books with favorite characters, there are Step into Reading Non-Fiction Readers, Phonics Readers and Boxed Sets, Sticker Readers, and Comic Readers—a complete literacy program with something to interest every child.

Learning to Read, Step by Step!

Ready to Read   Preschool–Kindergarten
• big type and easy words • rhyme and rhythm • picture clues
For children who know the alphabet and are eager to begin reading.

Reading with Help   Preschool–Grade 1
• basic vocabulary • short sentences • simple stories
For children who recognize familiar words and sound out new words with help.

Reading on Your Own   Grades 1–3
• engaging characters • easy-to-follow plots • popular topics
For children who are ready to read on their own.

Reading Paragraphs   Grades 2–3
• challenging vocabulary • short paragraphs • exciting stories
For newly independent readers who read simple sentences with confidence.

Ready for Chapters   Grades 2–4
• chapters • longer paragraphs • full-color art
For children who want to take the plunge into chapter books but still like colorful pictures.

STEP INTO READING® is designed to give every child a successful reading experience. The grade levels are only guides; children will progress through the steps at their own speed, developing confidence in their reading.

Remember, a lifetime love of reading starts with a single step!

Visit us on the Web!
StepIntoReading.com
randomhouse.com/kids

Educators and librarians, for a variety of teaching tools, visit us at RHTeachersLibrarians.com

ISBN 978-0-385-38447-6 (trade) — ISBN 978-0-385-38448-3 (lib. bdg.)
Printed in the United States of America
10 9 8 7 6 5 4 3 2 1

nickelodeon

CHASE IS ON THE CASE!

PAW PATROL

Based on the teleplay "Pups in a Fog"
by Carolyn Hay

Illustrated by Fabrizio Petrossi

Random House 🏠 New York

Ryder sees a problem
at the lighthouse.

The light is out.
Without it,
ships could crash
into Seal Island!

Captain Turbot calls
Ryder for help.

Captain Turbot cannot
find the lighthouse.
He is lost in the fog!

PAW Patrol is
ready for action!

"We need to fix
the lighthouse,"
Ryder tells the pups.

"Chase, I need
your searchlight,"
says Ryder.

10

"We will need
Zuma's hovercraft, too."

Ryder, Zuma, and Chase
race to Seal Island.

"We have to fix
that light,"
says Ryder.

Wally the walrus
is in the way!
"He wants a treat,"
says Ryder.

He throws a treat.

"Catch, Wally!"

Wally gulps it down.

Ryder, Zuma, and Chase
reach Seal Island.
A big ship is coming!

Chase is
on the case!
He will warn
the ship.

The lighthouse door
is locked!
Chase shoots out
his net.

Ryder climbs up the net.
Now he can go through
the window
and unlock the door.

Chase is in!
He turns on
his searchlight.

The big ship sees
Chase's light.
It turns away
from the rocks.
The ship is safe!

Captain Turbot follows
Chase's light.
He takes a new bulb
to the lighthouse.

The light is bright.

The lighthouse is fixed.

The PAW Patrol has

saved the day!

"Whenever you are
in trouble,
just yelp for help!"
Ryder says.